HOT CARS

DODGE CHARGER

FRANK GROUT

rourkeeducationalmedia.com

HOT CARS DODGE CHARGER

TABLE OF CONTENTS

Charging Ahead 4
The Look of Power 8
American Muscle Car............................ 10
The Charger and NASCAR.................... 15
The General Lee and Others 20
Charger History 24

HOT CARS   DODGE CHARGER

Charging Into the Future 29
Glossary... 30
Index 31
Show What You Know 31
Websites to Visit 31
About The Author 32

HOT CARS   DODGE CHARGER

CHARGING AHEAD

In the past, a charger was a term used to describe a horse trained for battle. Now, the word pretty much means "one cool car." Like its warhorse **namesake**, the 2016 Dodge Charger is powerful and flashy, able to conquer modern traffic rather than warriors.

HOT CARS   DODGE CHARGER

The 2016 Charger is able to shift from rear-wheel drive to all-wheel drive by itself without any input from the driver, depending on road conditions.

HOT CARS   DODGE CHARGER

The interior of the 2016 Dodge Charger is as cool as its exterior.

HOT CARS — DODGE CHARGER

The Look of Power

The 2016 Dodge Charger SRT Hellcat has sports-car style and muscle-car power. Long and sleek, the front of the Charger covers a killer 707-horsepower engine, making it the most powerful **sedan** ever made. The Hellcat is also the quickest sedan ever, able to go one-fourth of a mile (.4 kilometers) in just 11 seconds. In addition, it is the fastest sedan ever, reaching 204 miles (333 kilometers) per hour on a track.

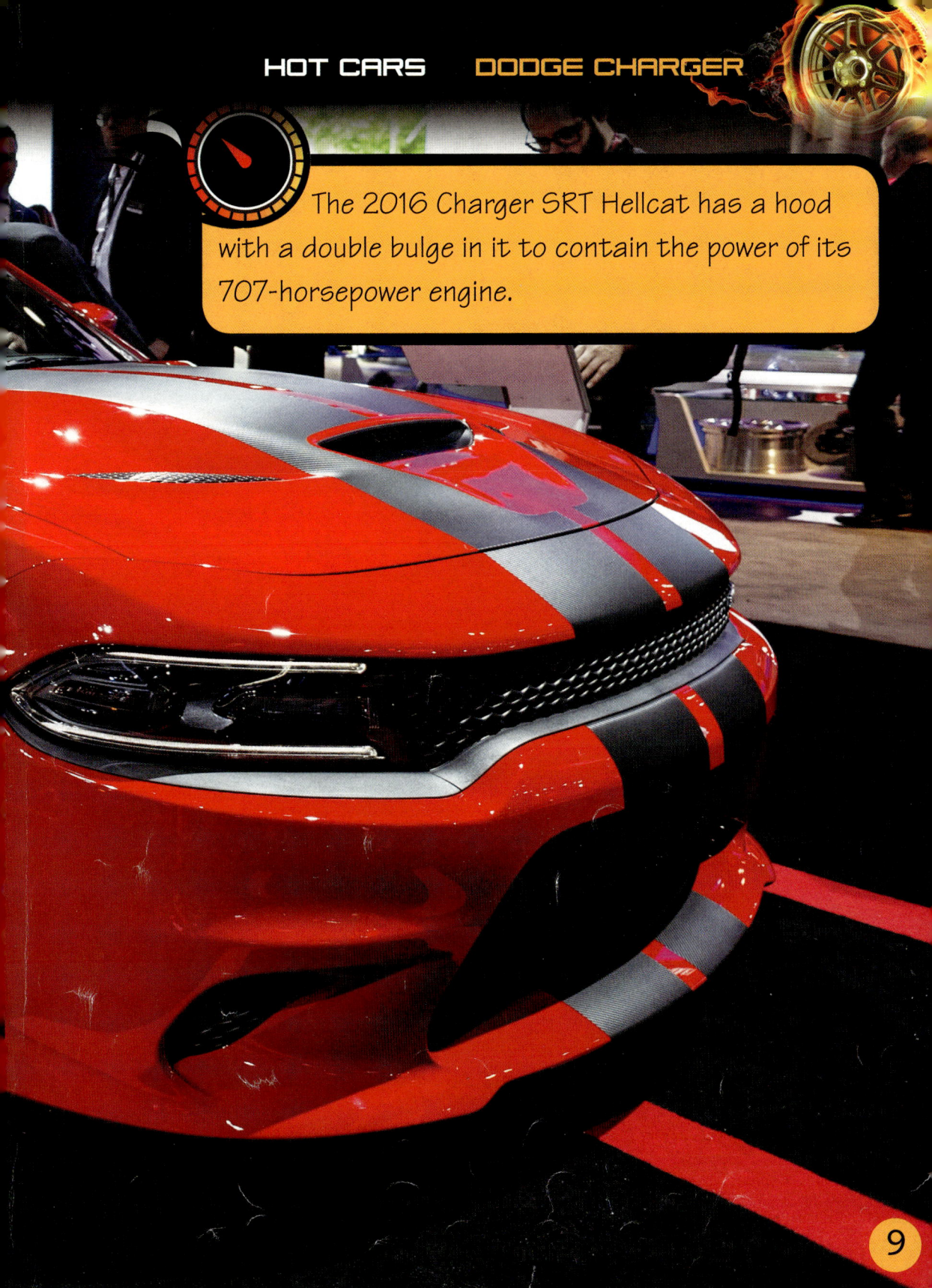

HOT CARS　　DODGE CHARGER

The 2016 Charger SRT Hellcat has a hood with a double bulge in it to contain the power of its 707-horsepower engine.

HOT CARS   DODGE CHARGER

American Muscle Car

Today's Charger comes from a long line of muscle cars. Muscle cars were lighter, two-door cars with powerful V-8 engines. They were made for street driving and occasional drag racing.

HOT CARS — DODGE CHARGER

The 1969 Dodge Charger Daytona was one of the most famous muscle cars ever made. It was one of the "Winged Warriors," a group of cars that included the Plymouth Superbird, Ford Torino Talladega, and the Mercury Cyclone Spoiler II. The Charger Daytona was named after Daytona Beach, Florida, a center for auto racing.

◀ 1969 Dodge Charger Daytona

The Ford Torino Talladega is named after the Talladega Superspeedway, formerly known as Alabama International Motor Speedway, a motorsports complex located north of Talladega, Alabama.

Besides the Charger, other famous muscle cars were the Chevy Corvette and the Ford Mustang. Most experts say the era of the muscle cars ended in 1973 when gasoline shortages and **emission** controls put the brake on cars that burned a lot of gasoline.

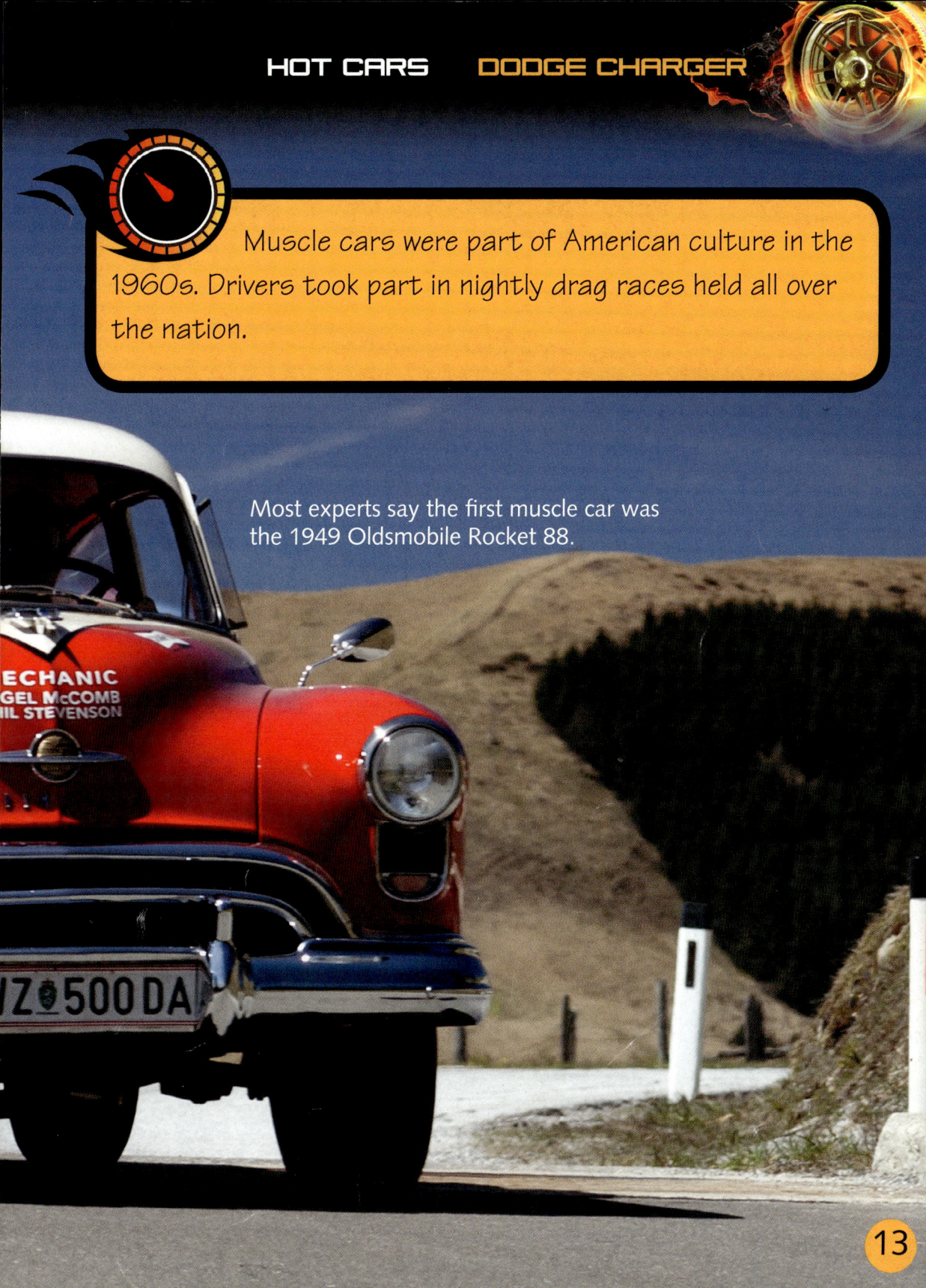

HOT CARS DODGE CHARGER

Muscle cars were part of American culture in the 1960s. Drivers took part in nightly drag races held all over the nation.

Most experts say the first muscle car was the 1949 Oldsmobile Rocket 88.

HOT CARS — DODGE CHARGER

Replica of Buddy Baker's 1969 Dodge Daytona

NASCAR stands for National Association for Stock Car Auto Racing.

HOT CARS   DODGE CHARGER

The Charger and NASCAR

The Dodge Charger has been a favorite of NASCAR drivers. A 1969 Dodge Daytona stock car driven by Buddy Baker in 1970 was the first stock car to go over 200 miles (321 kilometers) per hour on a race track.

HOT CARS   DODGE CHARGER

The first generation Dodge Daytona stock car had a huge spoiler in the back.

A stock car is an ordinary car specially **modified** for racing. The Charger Daytona has been called "the most **aerodynamic** stock car ever built." It has a low, pointed nose and a high spoiler, or safety stabilizer, mounted on its rear. It was quickly nicknamed "the winged thing."

HOT CARS   DODGE CHARGER

NASCAR racing is the No. 1 spectator sport in the United States in terms of the number of people who turn out to watch the races.

The second generation NASCAR Daytona dropped the huge spoiler and is closer to the ground.

HOT CARS — DODGE CHARGER

NASCAR legend Richard Petty won 25 races between 1972 and 1977 driving a 1972 Dodge Charger Daytona. Petty said the Charger is his all-time favorite stock car. He has won the Daytona 500 race a record seven times.

NASCAR sponsors more than 1,500 races at over 100 tracks in 39 states and in Canada. The sport is broadcast in 150 countries and is the second-most watched sport on television, after the National Football League (NFL).

Richard Petty's 1973 Dodge Charger ▶

HOT CARS — DODGE CHARGER

The General Lee and Others

Over the years, the Dodge Charger became known as one of the baddest muscle cars around. It's not surprising that the Charger was featured in movies and on TV.

Replica of the 1968/1969 Dodge Charger known as General Lee from the TV series, *The Dukes of Hazzard.*

HOT CARS   DODGE CHARGER

One of the most famous Chargers was The General Lee, known simply as "the general." The car was a star of *The Dukes of Hazzard*, a popular TV show that appeared on CBS from 1979 to 1985.

The car's name in *The Dukes of Hazzard* is a reference to American Civil War general Robert E. Lee. The idea for the General Lee was developed from a famous bootlegger's car.

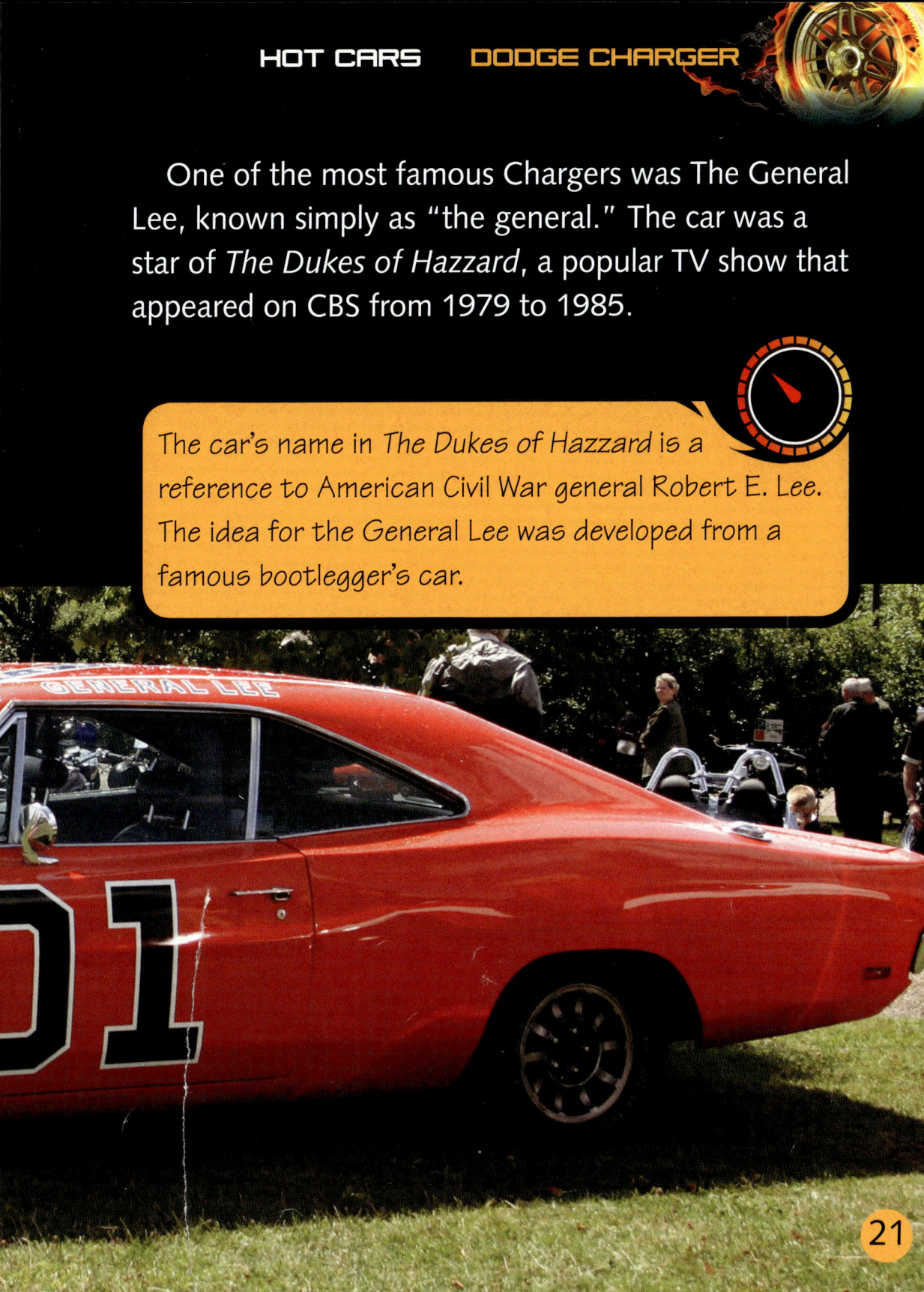

HOT CARS — DODGE CHARGER

Chargers also made it to the big screen in the movies *Bullitt* (1968), *Christine* (1983), *The Fast and the Furious* (2001), *The Dukes of Hazzard* (movie, 2005), *Death Proof*, (2007) and *Fast and Furious 6* (2013).

This Dodge Charger was outfitted for the Syfy TV series *Defiance*.

HOT CARS — DODGE CHARGER

Charger History

1966: The Dodge Charger is introduced. Total Charger production for 1966 was 37,344 cars.

1967: The Charger is fitted with the 440 Magnum engine rated at 375 horsepower.

1969: Dodge introduces the Charger Daytona.

1970: Dodge introduces the 440 Six Pack engine to the Charger featuring 390 horsepower.

The 1966 muscle car Charger had a killer grille in front.

HOT CARS   DODGE CHARGER

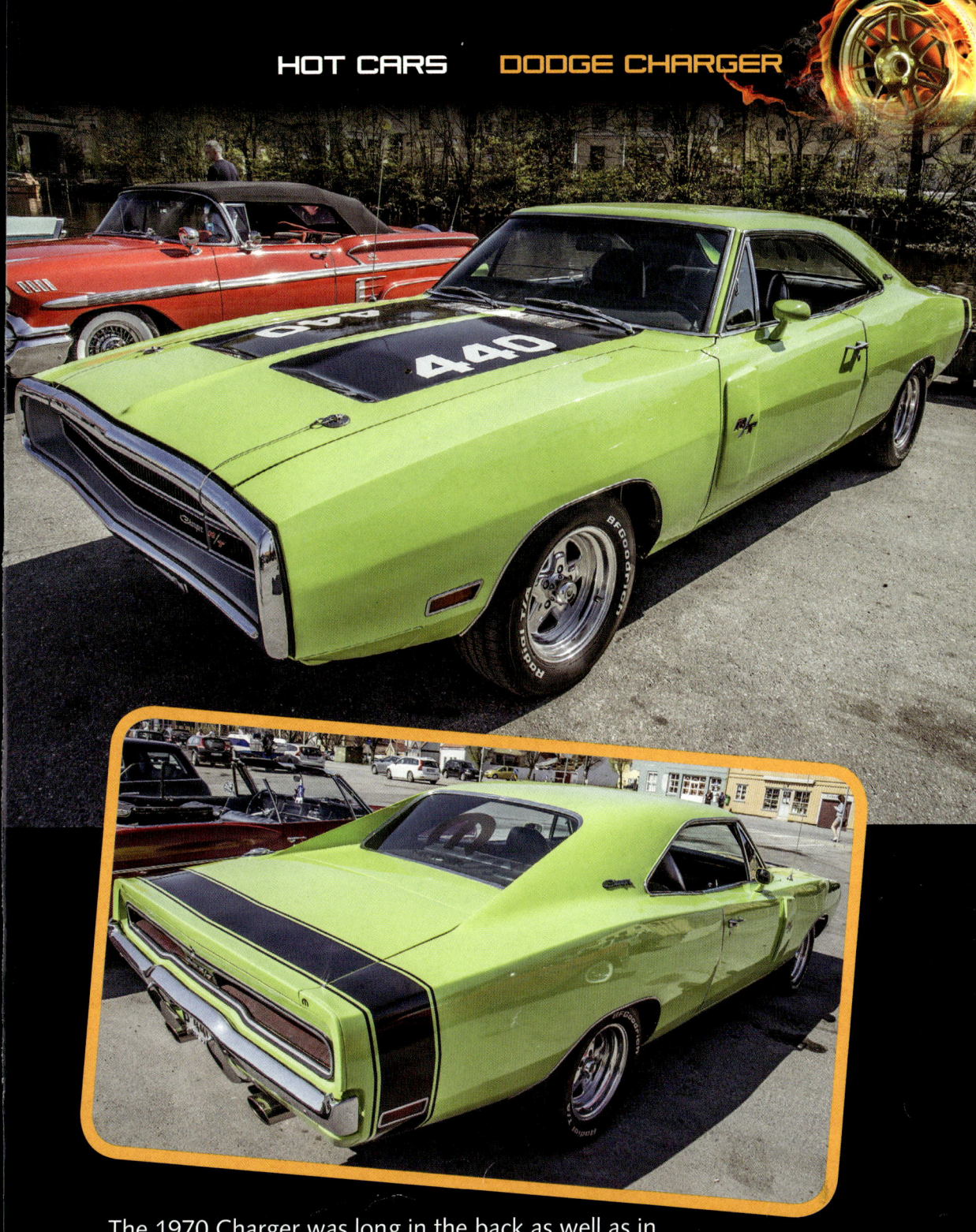

The 1970 Charger was long in the back as well as in the front.

HOT CARS   **DODGE CHARGER**

1975: No more muscle car. The Charger is redesigned to be a twin of the Chrysler Cordoba, a luxury car.

1978: Only 2,800 Chargers were produced as the Charger was discontinued and replaced by the 1978 Dodge Magnum.

1983: The Dodge Charger was returned to the Dodge lineup as a front wheel drive four-cylinder sedan.

Dodge sold more than 30,000 1975 model year Chargers.

HOT CARS   DODGE CHARGER

2005: Back to muscle. Dodge uses the Charger shape for its 2005 and 2006 NASCAR racing cars.

HOT CARS — DODGE CHARGER

2011: Dodge restyles the Charger's body and interior to reflect its 1968 to 1970 muscle cars. A new Pentastar engine (292 horsepower) replaces the car's older engine. Charger SRT-8 jumps from zero to 60 miles (96.5 kilometers) per hour in 4.3 seconds.

HOT CARS   DODGE CHARGER

Charging Into The Future

What's ahead for the Dodge Charger? Giant Italian car company Fiat owns Dodge. Fiat wants to combine the **heritage** of the Charger with the latest electronics and European styling. The new car for the future may be called Charger or Barracuda or Avenger. Whatever its name, however, it will be the latest in the muscle-car heritage established by the Dodge Charger.

Fiat bought Dodge and the remaining parts of Chrysler on January 21, 2014 for $3.5 billion.

GLOSSARY

aerodynamic (air-oh-dye-NAM-ik): designed to move through the air very easily and quickly

emission (i-MISH-uhn): the release of something, especially chemicals, into the atmosphere

heritage (HER-i-tij): traditions and beliefs

modified (MAH-duh-fyed): to change something in order to meet a specific need

namesake (NAME-sakh): something that has the name of something else

sedan (suh-dan): an enclosed automobile for four or more people, with two or four doors

INDEX

all-wheel drive 5
Baker, Buddy 14, 15
Daytona 500 18, 19
Daytona Speedway 19
Dodge Charger Daytona
    11, 18
Fiat 29
muscle car(s) 8, 10, 11, 12, 13,
    20, 24, 26, 28, 29
NASCAR 14, 15, 17, 18,
    19, 27
Oldsmobile Rocket 88 13
Pentastar engine 28
Petty, Richard 18,19
Talladega Superspeedway 11
The Dukes of Hazzard 20,
    21, 22
Winged Warriors 11

SHOW WHAT YOU KNOW

1. What did the word *charger* refer to before cars were invented?
2. What are two characteristics of muscle cars?
3. What cars belonged to the Winged Warriors?
4. What years was *The Dukes of Hazzard* on TV?
5. How long does it take the Charger SRT-8 to go from zero to 60 miles (96.5 kilometers) per hour?

WEBSITES TO VISIT

www.dodge.com/en/charger
www.edmunds.com/dodge/charger/history.html
www.carfax.com/blog/american-muscle-car-grew

ABOUT THE AUTHOR

Frank Grout comes from the Chicago area where he has lived all his life. He drove a used Dodge Charger as a teenager and fell in love with it. As an adult he bought a new Charger and, although it didn't replace his affections for his first Charger, he loves it, too. He was thrilled to write a book about the car he loves.

Meet The Author!
www.meetREMauthors.com

© 2017 Rourke Educational Media

All rights reserved. No part of this book may be reproduced or utilized in any form or by any means, electronic or mechanical including photocopying, recording, or by any information storage and retrieval system without permission in writing from the publisher.

www.rourkeeducationalmedia.com

PHOTO CREDITS: Cover © Trever Smith; Header art © Petrosg; speedometer art © diodes, both Shutterstock.com; pages 2-3 © Darren Brode-Shutterstock.com; pages 4-9 © Ed Aldridge-Shutterstock.com; PAGES 10-11 Dodge Charger Daytona © jeremyg3030 at http://flickr.com/photos/126433814@N04/16801306867, page 11 © Carl Sharp https://creativecommons.org/licenses/by-sa/3.0/deed.en; pages 12-13 © DeepGreen-Shutterstock.com; pages 14-15 © Royalbroil, https://creativecommons.org/licenses/by-sa/3.0/deed.en; page 16 © PSParrot from England, https://creativecommons.org/licenses/by/2.0/deed.en, page 17© Action Sports Photography-Shutterstock.com; page 18-19 © dodge challenger1 https://creativecommons.org/licenses/by/2.0/deed.en; pages 20-21 © Helen Shorey-Shutterstock.com, pages 22-23 © Steve Lagreca-Shutterstock.com; page 24 © Peeler37 | Dreamstime.com - <a href="http://www.dreamstime.com/editorial-image-dodge-charger-beautiful-industrial-area-image42336595#res1353349">1966 Dodge Charger Photo</a> ; page 25 © Steirus all Dreamstime.com; page 26 © Bull-Doser, page 27 © Liftarn https://creativecommons.org/licenses/by/2.0/deed.en; page 28 © Andrey Troitskiy | Dreamstime.com; page 32 author avatar © Yury Shchipakin, Shutterstock

Edited by: Keli Sipperley

Cover design by: Rhea Magaro
Interior design by: Nicola Stratford   www.nicolastratford.com

Library of Congress PCN Data

Dodge Charger / Frank Grout
   (*VROOM!* Hot Cars)
   ISBN 978-1-68191-748-1 (hard cover)
   ISBN 978-1-68191-849-5 (soft cover)
   ISBN 978-1-68191-940-9 (e-Book)
Library of Congress Control Number: 2016932711

Rourke Educational Media
Printed in the United States of America, North Mankato, Minnesota

Also Available as: